WALT DISNEY PRODUCTIONS'

the Fox and the Hound

LOST & FOUND

GOLDEN PRESS · NEW YORK

Western Publishing Company, Inc. · Racine, Wisconsin

TOD the fox was looking for his friend Copper.
But Copper wasn't anywhere near his barrel home.
"I'll just have to follow his trail," said Tod.

The little fox put his nose to the ground and tried to follow Copper's smell, but other smells kept getting in his way.

First Tod smelled the pine trees
where Big Mama the owl lived.
"Copper was here a little while
ago, honey," she told Tod,
"but he's gone now. Why don't
you try the apple orchard?"

The orchard was full of the smell of ripe apples. Dinky the sparrow was peering into a hole in one of them. "Where is that worm?" he was muttering. "He must be in there somewhere."

"Dinky won't be any help," thought Tod. "He's too busy trying to catch his lunch. I guess I'll look in the meadow for Copper."

Tod started across the meadow. It smelled green and grassy. Tod couldn't see Copper and he certainly couldn't smell him.

Soon Tod came to his own back yard. All he
could smell there were the chips of freshly cut
wood around the woodpile. "Where could Copper
be?" Tod wondered.

He sniffed at the patch of mint
growing beside the porch, then
went up the stairs into the kitchen.

Someone had spilled ginger all over the kitchen
floor. The sharp smell made Tod's eyes water.
He was rubbing them with his paw when he heard
a loud sneeze.

He looked across the room. There, sitting in
the middle of a pile of black pepper, was Copper.
"Oh, Tod," said Copper. "Look what I've done.
I came in here looking for you and I knocked
over Widow Tweed's spices."

Just then, Widow Tweed came into the kitchen. "Tod and Copper," she gasped. "You rascals! How could you? Shoo this minute!" She chased them out the kitchen door with her broom.

The two little friends hid under a lilac bush.
"I'm sorry, Tod," said Copper. "I got you in trouble.
Now what can we do?"

"I know," said Tod. "Those flowers smell really good.
Let's take some to Widow Tweed for a present."